Goethe Dies

THE
SEAGULL
LIBRARY OF
GERMAN
LITERATURE

Goethe Dies

THOMAS BERNHARD

TRANSLATED BY JAMES REIDEL

Seagull
BOOKS

LONDON NEW YORK CALCUTTA

This publication was supported by a grant
from the Goethe-Institut India

Seagull Books, 2019

Originally published as Thomas Bernhard, *Goethe schtirbt*.
Erzählungen © Suhrkamp Verlag Berlin, 2010

First published in English translation by Seagull Books, 2016
English translation © James Reidel, 2016

ISBN   978 0 8574 2 705 2

British Library Cataloguing-in-Publication Data
A catalogue record for this book is available from the British Library

Typeset by Seagull Books, Calcutta, India
Printed and bound by Hyam Enterprises, Calcutta, India

CONTENTS

Goethe Dies

In the late morning of the twenty-second he, Riemer, before my appointed visit with Goethe at half past two, warned me to *speak softly on one side, but not too softly on the other* with that man of whom it could be said is not only the greatest man in the nation but also the greatest German of all to this day, for he can now hear in the one ear *quite disturbingly clear while in the other almost virtually nothing at all any more*, and one never knows what he hears or what he does not, and the hardest part of holding a conversation with a man who lies on his deathbed, more or less motionless the whole time, a genius staring in the direction of the window, is to find the appropriate pitch in one's own voice, which was still possible, specifically through the most supreme mental effort of attentiveness, to find in this now simply depressing conversation indeed that precise midpoint which is still in accord with the mind of one who has arrived, for all to see, at his endpoint. He, Riemer, had spoken with Goethe several times in the

last three days, twice in the presence of Kräuter, whom
Goethe is said to have requested continuously, and up to
the last minute, to remain at his side, but alone at one
point as well, for Kräuter suddenly felt sick to his stomach,
due apparently to Riemer's presence in Goethe's bedchamber, and hurriedly took his leave, whereupon
Goethe promptly began discussing with Riemer, just as
in days past, *The Doubting and the Doubting Nothing*, just as
in those first days of March during which Goethe, thus
said Riemer, kept coming back to this subject time and
time again and with this utmost vigilance time and time
again to the virtual exclusion of anything else since the
end of February, for he had, thus said Riemer, on his daily
morning constitutional with Riemer, as it were, hence
without Kräuter and, hence from Riemer again, without
that *evil familiar* regarded as *the Lier-in-Wait of this Goethean
death*, been preoccupied with the *Tractatus Logico-philosophicus* and even referred to the body of Wittgensteinian
thought as that *which stood at once alongside his first*, as well
as *that which superseded his*, specifically at the point where
the decision came between that which Goethe had been
compelled for a lifetime to observe and record as Here
and that which he had as There for a lifetime would have
to be eclipsed ultimately, if not *completely eclipsed*, by
Wittgensteinian thought. With time Goethe allegedly
worked himself up over the notion, as Kräuter confirmed,
of summoning Wittgenstein from England to Weimar
under any circumstances and as soon as possible and Kräuter

would in effect be bringing Wittgenstein to see Goethe
oddly enough on this, the twenty-second; the   idea of
inviting Wittgenstein to Weimar occurred to Goethe at
the end of February, thus said Riemer presently, and not
at the beginning of March, as Kräuter maintained, and it
was Kräuter who learnt from Eckermann that   Eckermann would prevent Wittgenstein from travelling to
Weimar to see Goethe at all costs; Eckermann gave Goethe
a recital about Wittgenstein, thus said Kräuter, with an
impertinence such that Goethe, still in full possession of   his
faculties as well as being physically able on a day-by-day
capacity to go into town, hence leaving the house in the
Frauenplan entirely for the neighbourhood where
Wieland lived by way of the Schiller house, thus said
Riemer, such that Goethe refused to hear another word
from Eckermann about Wittgenstein, *that most venerable of
men* as Goethe allegedly said word for word, and then
Goethe allegedly said to Eckermann that his services,
which he, Eckermann, had always thus far performed for
him, for Goethe, in these days and in this saddest of hours
in the history of German philosophy, were null and void,
for he, Eckermann, had perfidiously maligned Wittgenstein
in front of Goethe, had made himself unforgivably guilty,
and had to leave the room at once, *The room*, Goethe
allegedly said, which was quite out of character for him
since he always called his bedroom *The bedchamber*, and
then suddenly he, thus said Riemer, flung the word *room*
at Eckermann's head, and Eckermann stood there for a

moment completely speechless, not getting a word out, thus said Riemer, and left Goethe. *He wanted to take from me my most sacred thing,* Goethe allegedly said to Riemer, *he, Eckermann, who owes everything to me, to whom I have given everything and who, Riemer, would be nothing without me.* After Eckermann left the bedchamber, Goethe was incapable of saying a word, but he did allegedly say the word *Eckermann,* so often indeed that it seemed to Riemer as though Goethe were on the verge of going mad. But then Goethe quickly mastered himself and, without one word more about Eckermann, was able to speak to Riemer of only Wittgenstein. It meant the greatest providence to him, Goethe, to know that his closest confidante was in Oxford, separated only by the Channel, thus said Riemer, which frankly seems to me highly plausible in this account, one which is more often than not everywhere else rhapsodic, unbelievable; but then suddenly Riemer's narrative took on an authenticity which usually escaped me in his other reports, Wittgenstein in Oxford, Goethe allegedly said, Goethe in Weimar, such a serendipitous thought, dear Riemer, who can know the value of this thought but I myself, who is the luckiest of men in this thought. Riemer underscored that Goethe allegedly said *The luckiest* several times. In regard to Wittgenstein in Oxford. When Riemer said, *In Cambridge,* Goethe allegedly said, *Oxford or Cambridge, it is the most serendipitous thought of my life and this life has been filled with serendipitous thoughts.* Of all these happy thoughts is the thought that Wittgenstein is my happiest. Riemer, not knowing at first to make the connection between Goethe and Wittgenstein, spoke with Kräuter, who, like Ecker- mann, wanted to know nothing about Wittgenstein being in Weimar. While Goethe, as I know from remarks Goethe made to me, wanted to see Wittgenstein as soon as possible, Kräuter spoke continuously of how Wittgenstein could *not come before April*, and that March is a most inopportune time, even Goethe doesn't realize this, but he, Kräuter, knows that Eckermann, for many reasons, wasn't altogether wrong to talk Goethe out of Wittgenstein, which was pointless, of course, as Kräuter told me, since Goethe had never let him- self be talked out of anything by Eckermann, but Ecker- mann always had good intuition, as Kräuter told me while walking past Wieland's house; Eckermann, on the day in question, the day on which Goethe unequivocally asked for Wittgenstein, for a personal appearance by his succes- sor, so to speak, had gone too far, he, Eckermann, on that day had simply underestimated Goethe's mental and phys- ical strength as well as competence, and Goethe severed himself from Eckermann over Wittgenstein, over nothing other than that. An attempt made by the women downstairs (who stood in the hall!) in persuading Goethe from not going through with his intention, which, of course, had already become this final decision, of actually chasing off Eckermann for ever in favour of Wittgenstein, something the women could not comprehend naturally, had failed to, and for two days, as I know, Goethe did indeed forbid any women at all from visiting his bedchamber, even though Goethe, as I said to Riemer, had never managed without women for a single day in his life; meanwhile Eckermann, as Kräuter said later, had allegedly been standing downstairs with the women in the hall dumbstruck while they, allegedly, besieged him, so to speak, over the issue of Goethe's terrible condition, the entire extent of which hadn't been taken seriously, not as seriously, anyway, as Eckermann should have taken it at the time and one of the women from the many standing in the hall, I no longer know which, approached Goethe to stand up for Eckermann, but Goethe was no longer persuadable, he allegedly said that he had never been so disappointed by any living person and in such a most insensitive manner as he had by Eckermann, and he wanted to see him no more. Goethe's *no more* had often been heard in the hall, even after Eckermann had long been gone from Goethe's household and was indeed seen no more. No one knows where he is now. Kräuter made enquiries, but all these enquiries proved inconclusive. Even the police in Halle and Leipzig were engaged, thus said Riemer, and Kräuter had also furnished news of Eckermann's disappearance in Berlin and Vienna, thus said Riemer. In fact, Kräuter, thus said Riemer, had tried several times to dissuade Goethe from the idea of summoning Wittgenstein to Weimar, and it wasn't certain if, thus said Kräuter, Wittgenstein would really come to Weimar even if he were invited by Goethe, by the greatest of Germans, for Wittgenstein's thought, in any case, made that certainty unpredictable, thus said Kräuter word for word, but then again, he, Kräuter, thus said Riemer, warned Goethe of Wittgenstein being in Weimar with uncommon tactfulness and without coming on so clumsily familiar as Eckermann truly had, who had simply gone too far in this Wittgenstein business, since he had been so self-assured in this matter, since he hadn't realized that one can never be too sure of Goethe's thoughts and ideas under any circumstances, thus proving that Eckermann until the last could not shed what *we know about Eckermann, his mental limitations*, thus said Riemer, but even Kräuter was unsuccessful in dissuading Goethe from summoning Wittgenstein to Weimar. A telegram is not sent to such an intellect, Goethe allegedly said, one simply cannot invite such an intellect via telegraph, one needs to send an emissary bodily to England is what Goethe allegedly said to Kräuter. To which Kräuter allegedly said nothing and since Goethe was determined to see Wittgenstein *face to face*, as Riemer now loftily said, for Kräuter allegedly said it in the exact same lofty way, and in the end Kräuter had to submit to Goethe's wish despite how hard as it was for him. Goethe allegedly said that if he had been in better health, he would have travelled to Oxford or Cambridge himself to converse with Wittgenstein about *The Doubting and the Doubting Nothing*, going to meet Wittgenstein mattered not to him, moreover, if the Germans simply do not understand such an idea, he, Goethe, would totally disregard it, as he always dismissed every thought of the Germans, especially since he was *the* German, what would be totally natural of him to say, *I would like to go to England at the end of my life*, Goethe allegedly said to Kräuter, but my powers are no longer sufficient, so I am forced to propose to Wittgenstein that he come to me. *Of course*, Goethe allegedly said to Kräuter, *Wittgenstein, my philosophical son, so to speak*, thus said Kräuter, who vouches for the veracity of Goethe's statement, *will stay at my house. And, indeed, in the most comfortable of all the rooms we have. I will furnish the room as well in a way which I think Wittgenstein will like. And if he stays for two days, I could want nothing better!* Goethe allegedly cried out. Kräuter, thus said Riemer, was aghast at these rather specific requests made by Goethe. He excused himself and left Goethe's room for at least a few minutes to inform the women in the hall downstairs and even in the kitchen of Goethe's intention of inviting Wittgenstein to stay at his house. Of course, these females had no idea who Wittgenstein is, Kräuter allegedly said to Riemer, thus said Riemer. They thought Kräuter had gone mad. Wittgenstein is a most important man to Goethe, Kräuter allegedly told the kitchen ladies, whereupon they took him to be crazy. Once more Kräuter went through Goethe's household and said *Wittgenstein is of utmost importance to Goethe* and everyone who hears this needs to get it into their head. *An Austrian thinker!* Kräuter allegedly shouted at the physician who attended to Goethe and came twice daily, whereupon this physician (I shall not mention his name so that he cannot bring me to court!) allegedly said to Kräuter that he, Kräuter, had gone insane, whereupon Kräuter allegedly said to the physician that he, the physician, was the one insane, whereupon the physician allegedly retorted that Kräuter belonged in Bedlam, where- upon Kräuter allegedly said to the physician that he belonged in Bedlam, and so forth. Finally, Kräuter thought that Goethe in the meantime had calmed down about this idea of inviting Wittgenstein to Weimar and even into his house, and, in time, once more entered Goethe's room. The genius, thus said Riemer, Kräuter allegedly said, now stood at the window contemplating an ice-covered dahlia in the garden. *Look here, Kräuter, at this ice-covered dahlia*! Goethe allegedly exclaimed and his voice was as strong as ever, *This is the Doubting and the Doubting Nothing*! Goethe allegedly remained standing at the window for a long time and then gave Kräuter the task of finding and inviting Wittgenstein from (it mattered not where really!) Oxford or Cambridge. I believe the Channel is frozen over and that means you should bundle yourself up in a proper fur! Goethe allegedly told Kräuter. Wrap yourself in a proper fur and search for Wittgenstein and invite him to Weimar for the twenty-second of March. It's my dying wish, Kräuter, to see Wittgenstein precisely on the twenty-second of March. I have no other wish. If Schopenhauer and Stifter were still alive, I would invite them both along with Wittgenstein, but Schopenhauer and Stifter are no longer alive, so I will only invite

Wittgenstein. And when I think of it just now, thus said Goethe at the window, with his right hand supported by his cane, Wittgenstein is the greatest of all. Kräuter, thus said Riemer, allegedly remarked to Goethe about the difficulty of travelling *from England during this cold and inhospitable time of year, through half of Germany and across the Channel to London and beyond.* Dreadful, Goethe! Kräuter allegedly exclaimed, thus said Riemer, followed by Goethe with as much forcefulness: *Go, Kräuter, go*! Whereupon Kräuter, thus said Riemer with his infamous schadenfreude, with nothing else remaining, turned around and left on his journey. The women made a terrible fuss over him. They brought an entire procession of fur capes from Goethe's possessions, about two dozen, among them the fur travelling cape of Cornelia Schellhorn which Goethe had kept and had never removed *from its sacred place*, and among them as well, thus said Riemer, a fur of Katharina Elisabeth Schultheiss, and, at last, one which Ernst August had forgotten at Goethe's, and Kräuter finally decided on this one, since it, according to Kräuter, thus said Riemer, would be the right one to wear on this journey to England. Finally, within two hours, Kräuter arrived at the train station and departed. Now Riemer had time with Goethe, as he said, and Goethe entrusted him, Riemer, with much about Kräuter, and also about Eckermann and others, things which did not put them in a good light. Thus Goethe complained, thus said Riemer, about Kräuter soon after his departure for

England, that this man, Kräuter, had always neglected Goethe. Goethe didn't explain specifically how, nor did Riemer to me, but Goethe continuously spoke to Riemer, using the word *neglected* in reference to Kräuter. Even though Kräuter is a stupid man, as Goethe allegedly said over and over again to Riemer, Eckermann is *stupider still*. Ernst August had not been the great Ernst August everyone took him to be now. *He was stupider*, Goethe allegedly said, *lower than one knows*. He also allegedly referred to Ulrike *as stupid*. And Madame von Stein and her salon. He destroyed Kleist, something for which he was not sorry. Riemer could grasp nothing, but I think I know what Goethe meant. Wieland, Herder, he esteemed much higher than in his dealings with them. *In the wind snick the weathervanes*, Goethe allegedly said, *where does that come from?* Riemer had no idea, I said from Hölderlin, but Riemer only shook his head. He, Goethe, thus said Riemer, had ruined the national theatre, and Goethe allegedly said that he, Goethe, had absolutely run German theatre into the ground, but people will still come to it for the next two hundred years. *What I have penned is undoubtedly the greatest, but I have also crippled German literature for a couple of centuries. I was, my dear man*, as Goethe allegedly said to Riemer, *a crippler of German literature*. They have all landed on the birdlime of my *Faust*. In the end, everything, even as great as it is, has only been *an omission* of my innermost feelings, a fraction of them all, as Riemer related, but in none of them was I the highest of all. Riemer believed that

Goethe was speaking of someone else altogether, not about himself, then he said to Riemer: *Therefore I have played an optical illusion on the German people, who are suited to this like no other. And to such a degree!* he allegedly shouted, the genius. Solemnly and with a lowered head, Goethe alleg-edly contemplated the portrait of Schiller on his nightstand and said: *I destroyed him with all my might, I deliberately destroyed him, made him sick first and then destroyed him. He wanted to be like me. The poor man! A house on the Esplanade, as I have one in the Frauenplan! What a mistake! For that I'm sorry,* Goethe allegedly said and was silent for a long time. It's a good thing, said Riemer, that Schiller can no longer hear this. Goethe allegedly held the portrait before his eyes and said: *I'm sorry for all the feeble efforts, that which can never measure up, because they haven't got the breath!* Thereupon, he allegedly set Schiller's portrait, which a lady friend of Wieland had painted for Goethe, back down on his nightstand. *What comes after me will have it hard,* Goethe allegedly said then. During this time, Kräuter was already well underway. We heard nothing from him save that he had purchased a relic of Bach in Magdeburg, a lock of the Thomaskantor's hair, which he wanted to bring back to Goethe upon his return. It's a good thing, said Riemer, that Kräuter was absent from Goethe's circle during this time. That way we could talk quite undisturbed, and for once Goethe would be without that demon and nonentity. As he had cut off Eckermann, thus said Riemer, so would he cut off Kräuter too. In regard to the women, thus said Riemer, they no longer play a role in his life now. It is philosophy, no more literature. One often sees him in the cemetery, it is as if he were searching for a plot there, and I always run into him at the plot which, to my taste, is the best one. Sheltered from the wind, totally isolated from everybody else. I had no inkling, thus said Riemer now on the Esplanade, of what suddenly brought on that morning's agitation, such that Goethe entered his final days. When I am with him again this evening, thus said Riemer in respect to Goethe, I will ask him to expound further about *The Doubting and the Doubting Nothing. We will organize this topic and*, thus said Goethe always, *attack and destroy it.* Everything he has read and thought until now is either nothing or *almost nothing* when compared to the Wittgensteinian. He no longer knows *who or what brought him to Wittgenstein. Perhaps that small booklet bound in a red cover from the Suhrkamp Library*, Goethe once told Riemer, thus said Riemer, *I can't say any more than that. But it was my lifesaver.* Hopefully, as Goethe said to Riemer, thus said Riemer, Kräuter will come through in Oxford or Cambridge and soon Wittgenstein will come. Allegedly, Goethe spent all day in his bedchamber and, as Riemer thinks, simply waited for Wittgenstein. And that is what happened, he simply waited for Wittgenstein, who is to him the one man and thing highest, thus said Riemer. He had slipped the *Tractatus* under his pillow. *The tautology has no truth-conditions, for it is unconditionally true; and the contradiction is on no condition true*, so he, Goethe, often said trembling in these days. From Karlsbad, allegedly, came wishes for his recovery, from Marienbad as well, and someone from lovely Elenbogen sent Goethe a glass painting in which he had been portrayed together with Wittgenstein. No one knows how they knew in Elen-bogen that Goethe and Wittgenstein are a pair, thus said Riemer, a pair in a glass painting. A beautiful glass painting. From Sicily a professor who lives in Agrigento sent an invitation for Goethe to come see his collection of Goethe's manuscripts. Goethe wrote to the professor that he was no longer capable of crossing the Alps, *even though he preferred their light more than the sound of the sea.* Goethe had completely retreated into his correspondence, thus said Riemer, into a kind of philosophizing, farewell correspondence. He wrote to a certain Edith Lafontaine in Paris, who had sent him her poems for his opinion, that she should turn to Voltaire, for that one had taken over the office of answering begging letters of a literary nature. The proprietor of the Hotel Pupp in Karlsbad had proposed to Goethe if he, Goethe, wouldn't like to purchase his hotel for 800,000 thalers, as it is said, minus the staff. As for the rest, the usual tasteless and vulgar mail arrived at the Frauenplan day in and day out, put into order by the secretaries and tossed out by Goethe, not by his hand, thus said Riemer, but by Kräuter or myself, and, best of all, it certainly was a good thing we had so many large tile stoves in which we could throw away these worthless, intrusive and utterly insensible letters. Suddenly, all of Germany believed it could turn to Goethe by letter, without exception. Every day Eckermann carried bushel baskets of letters to the various stoves. In this way, Goethe was kept warm most of the time with the mail he received in his last year. But back to Wittgenstein. Kräuter had, as Riemer now related to me, actually made it to Wittgenstein. However, this man had died of cancer the day before Kräuter called on him. He, Kräuter, thus said Riemer, had only seen Wittgenstein laid out on his bier. A haggard man with a gaunt face. Among the people around Wittgenstein, not one knew anything at all of Goethe. So Krauter left dejected once more. The big question now, thus said Riemer, was whether to tell Goethe of Wittgenstein's death. It was at this very minute that I said to Riemer, walking past the Schiller house, making our way back to the dying Goethe, who was now being nursed by his women, how I ought to be picking up Wittgenstein from the train station, at this very minute. Riemer looked at his watch, while I wanted to express the following: no one, save Goethe, wanted Wittgenstein to come to Weimar more than I did. It would have been the high point of my existence, I said *existence* where Goethe would have said *life*. Always, where Goethe said *life*, I said *existence*, it had been that way in Karlsbad, in Rostock, in Frankfurt, on Rügen, in Elenbogen. Even if Wittgenstein and Goethe just stood facing each other or sitting, remaining silent the whole time, and even if it had been the briefest of moments, it would have been the most beautiful moment that I could imagine, to which I bore witness. Riemer said that Goethe had set the *Tractatus above his Faust and above everything he wrote and thought*. This too is Goethe, said Riemer. He too is such a man. Yesterday morning, the twenty-first, as Riemer entered Goethe's room, as he said now, he found to his, to Riemer's surprise, Kräuter standing there, showing to this bedridden man, with four bolsters embroidered by Ulrike already supporting his head as in that official image of Goethe on his bier fittingly raised even higher, a small stunted hand and three fanatically outstretched fingers which meant with terrifying ruthlessness that he, Goethe, had only *three* more days left and not one more (in which he, Kräuter, was ultimately fooled!), while Goethe at first only said the Gickelhahn is to blame, several times Goethe allegedly said *the Gickelhahn is to blame*. Kräuter, still recovering from his mission to England, thus said Riemer, allegedly dipped a cloth in cold water, from a washbasin on a white-painted kitchen chair standing by the window, and wrung the cloth out for so long over the washbasin that it seemed to Riemer like an eternity, one of Kräuter's doing, thus said Riemer, the time being drawn out to a really outrageous length. While Kräuter wrung out the cloth over the washbasin, Goethe, already very weak, thus said Riemer, stared out the window into the garden, while he, Riemer, stood in the doorway of Goethe's bedchamber. He didn't have the will, thus said Riemer, to tell Goethe that Wittgenstein wasn't coming,

and Kräuter as well had been guarded about giving
Goethe this terrible news, neither could tell him Wittgenstein was long dead. And even though the people around
Wittgenstein knew nothing of Goethe, Kräuter, so as to
spare Goethe, for he, Kräuter, had been asked more than
once, answered Goethe: *Everyone knew Goethe, everyone.*
This had a rather pleasing effect on Goethe. At first
Goethe hadn't noticed that Riemer had entered the bedchamber and he calmly said to Kräuter: that if he could
choose now among all the people he had encountered
during his life (not *during his existence!*), indeed, among all
of those people he might want to have at his bedside now,
he could only utter the name *Eckermann*, something
which naturally surprised us, Kräuter and me, thus said
Riemer. At the name Eckermann, which Goethe suddenly, calmly uttered once more, Kräuter felt terror and
turned his back on Goethe. This remark seemed that of
someone losing his mind to me, thus said Riemer now.
Kräuter, isn't that Riemer there? Goethe suddenly asked,
whereupon Goethe gave me a look, thus said Riemer, but
this time it was different. It was clear to me that this day,
the twenty-second, would be Goethe's last. Eight days had
gone by since Wittgenstein had died. Now, he too, I
thought. Kräuter later confessed to me that he as well had
thought likewise at the same time. Then Kräuter pressed
the cool, moist cloth on Goethe's forehead *in this repul-
sively theatrical way*, thus said Riemer, *something we expect
from Kräuter. And from Eckermann as well.* Then, thus said

Riemer, Goethe said that he, who in building himself up to be so great, as he was now, had utterly destroyed everything else near him and around him. He hadn't lifted up Germany but had destroyed it. The eyes of the world, however, are blind to these thoughts. He, Goethe, drew on everything he had in order to annihilate, to create misery in the deepest sense. Systematically. *The Germans adore me, even though I have shamed them for centuries to come like no one else.* Kräuter vouched that Goethe made this remark quite calmly. The whole time, thus said Riemer, I had the impression Goethe had engaged an actor from the National Theatre to serve as his last caretaker when he subjected himself to Kräuter and I thought that he, Goethe, watched while Kräuter performed his role at Goethe's side in this way, as he pressed the cloth to Goethe's forehead, saw how Kräuter stood there when Goethe said: *I am the destroyer of the Germans!* quickly followed by: *and I don't have a bad conscience!*, while he placed Goethe's hand, for Goethe no longer had the strength to do so, a little higher on the bedspread in accordance with his, Kräuter's, aestheticism, thus said Riemer, but it wasn't perfect, for both of Goethe's hands came together like a corpse, something even Kräuter must have felt to be in bad taste while Kräuter finally wiped a bead of sweat from Goethe's face and pressed such an altogether disgusting pettiness on a day which to him, Riemer, should at least be painful, if not mortally wounding; for it was possible that such a depraved person as Kräuter was now a match to a mind such as Goethe, whom we must see not only as a great man, but very likely in fact the greatest in the end, that Kräuter, with his perfidy and charlatanism, had been empowered to rise in the strongest terms to the level of such a mental giant as Goethe when he had come to his end. To the furthest extent of treason, thus said Riemer. *Wittgenstein isn't staying at the Elephant,* Goethe allegedly still said, even as he laid on his deathbed already, *but in my house, right next to my bedroom. There is no other room suitable. I want Wittgenstein next to mine*! Goethe allegedly said to Riemer. When Goethe died on the twenty-second, it immediately occurred to me what a fateful coincidence it was that Goethe had invited Wittgenstein to Weimar on that exact day. What a sign from heaven. *The Doubting and the Doubting Nothing*, Goethe allegedly said, *before* the last thing. Thus a Wittgensteinian phrase. And then, shortly afterwards these two words which are his most famous, *More light*! In reality, however, Goethe's last words, however, were not *More light* but rather *No more*! Only Riemer and I—and Kräuter—were present. We, Riemer, Kräuter and I agreed to tell the world Goethe had said *More light* as his last words and not *No more*! I still suffer this lie as alteration, long after Riemer and Kräuter died of it, to this very day.

Montaigne:

A Story in Twenty-Two Instalments

From my family and thus from my tormentors, I found refuge in a corner of the tower and had, without light and thus without the mosquitoes driving me insane, brought with me a book from the library after I had read a few sentences in it, by Montaigne as it turned out, to whom I am related in such a close and truly enlightening way as I am to no one else.

On the way into the tower, I had, as though nothing could have saved me otherwise by doing so, pulled a book from the shelves in the gloom of the library without the faintest idea what the book would be about except that it was very likely philosophical, I thought, since my family for centuries had always shelved such so-called philosophical books on the left side of the library, and, of course, fully aware that I hadn't taken a so-called belletristic book from the right side of the library but rather from the left, therefore, none from the belletristic side but rather one of those from the philosophical side, even though I couldn't know what kind of philosophy it was when I pulled it down from the left side because it could have really been quite different from the one I ultimately did pull down, not Montaigne but rather Descartes or Novalis or Schopenhauer.

On the way into the tower, in which, as I said, I made no light given the mosquitoes, nevertheless I exerted the most intense concentration so as to guess whose book I had pulled from the shelf, but those who ran through my head in the process were all philosophers, just not Montaigne.

Since no one had gone from the library into the tower for so long, I soon plunged my head into hundreds of cobwebs and in the end, before I had even arrived at the tower, I felt as though I wore a cap of cobwebs. So thickly had the cobwebs wound around my head on the way from the library into the tower that I felt the cobwebs on my face and my head like a bandage, one I had wound around myself on the way from the library into the tower by walking alone and by repeatedly turning my head from side to side and my body entirely around because I was afraid that my family might have seen me first entering the library and then leaving the library in the direction of the tower. Even to breathe was difficult for me.

Now I had a fear of suffocating due to the many years in which I suffered alone with my weakened lungs, as well as another fear, one more excruciating still, from the cobwebs winding around my head. That whole after-noon, my family had tormented me with their business affairs and, while they continually talked on and on at me or treated me with total silence, no matter what had been discussed, they reproached me because I was their mis-fortune; that I had made it my method to be against them and their relationships, against their affairs and their ideas, which were my own as well.

That I made it my habit to undermine their thinking, to mock it, destroy and exterminate it. That I enlisted everything at my command to undermine it and destroy and exterminate it. I dwelt on nothing else day and night and, when I woke up, I worked against it. They said I was not the invalid and thus the weak one but rather that they were the invalids and the weak ones, I had tyrannized over them and not the other way around: I was their oppressor, not them against me but me against them.

But I will hear this for as long as I exist. From birth I was against them, holding my very existence against them as this wicked, never-speaking child just perpetually staring at them, their perfidious monstrosity. And from the very first this watchful child unsettled them because it had been against them. Instinctively, from the very first, everything in me turned against them, and ultimately, with the onset of a brain in my head, with ever-greater determination and ruthlessness.

I am their destroyer, they said once more today while
I, however, relentlessly convey that they are my destroyers,
committed to my destruction ever since I had been con-
ceived. My family has me on their conscience, in each and
everything I say, while they reciprocate in each and everything which they say and think, and in their relentless
dealings, such that I would have them on my conscience.
They incessantly tell me that I was born into such a fine
neighbourhood and into such a fine home, and that I
mocked and scorned them relentlessly.

In every one of my statements there was nothing but
this mockery and scorn in which they will one day perish,
but I think that one day I will perish in their mockery
and scorn. On the way from the library to the tower I
realized that I have not escaped them in all my forty-two
years, even though in these forty-two years I have had
nothing else in my head but to escape them. Withdrawing
myself from them was never possible. Not even for the
briefest time did I withdraw myself from them since it
would have been merely a token withdrawal, not to mention escape, to which I no longer lend credence. Their
care had always been the most considerate, their attention
always the greatest, but at the same time their despair in
regard to me was always the most appalling.

So many paths they had paved for me and I had taken
not a single one of these paths, as I told them once more
today. All the paths they had pointed out for me and
paved, which were the best for me, all these paths they

already saw me taking, but all their paths for me would have destroyed me from the outset. I said to them once that I never wanted to take a path, but their misunderstanding and, together with this misunderstanding, their thoroughgoing vulgarity in this most unabashed conspiracy, made me see instantly the absurdity of my remark, and I didn't let myself repeat this remark, that I never wanted to take a path. Every remark of mine was met by their misunderstanding and with this misunderstanding their assiduous vulgarity. Thus over the decades I have said less and less and finally nothing more, and their lectures have become evermore ruthless.

I had gone into the library and pulled a philosophy book off the shelves for myself in the full knowledge of committing a crime because in their eyes just going into the library was a crime and for that much greater crime of taking a philosophy book off the shelves, but where my withdrawal from them was still the only thing which counted as a crime. They said that they had bought a house in Encknach in order to enlarge it and then, in a year, sell it at a tenfold profit, they said that they had combined two farms in Rutzenmoos and made a profit of thirty million overnight. We must buy when the weak are at their weakest, they said at the table, beat the intelligent with a more ruthless intelligence, they said, with a more perfidious perfidy. They don't discuss these business deals directly, but only indirectly, even when they discuss something they see as philosophical, namely, the loneliness of

Schopenhauer, about which they have indeed, as I know, read everything but understand nothing, they really only discuss their business, how to cheat intelligence with a more intelligent intelligence. They spooned their soup and came to the defence of a dog which had bitten a passer-by and in this canine cant they nevertheless were still only talking about their business. My parents and my siblings have always been united, they have always acted in a conspiracy against everything and against me. We have always loved you, my parents said again today, and my siblings watched and listened to them without objection while I thought that they had only hated me all my life, just as I hated them all my life, when I speak the truth which I know and do not lie, against which I have struggled for a long time. Of course, we say that we love our parents but in reality we hate them, as we cannot love our begetters because we are not a happy people, and our unhappiness is not something talked into, like our happiness, which we talk ourselves into daily such that we always have the courage to get up, wash ourselves, dress, take the first sip, swallow the first bite.

Inevitably we are reminded of this every morning, that our parents made and whelped us in this horrific self-esteem and in their literal megalomania for breeding and put us in this more dreadful and odious and deadly than encouraging and conducive world. We owe our helplessness to our begetters, our awkwardness, every one of our difficulties which for a lifetime we can never overcome.

First it was said that you could not drink this water because it is poisoned, then it was said that you could not read this book because this book is poisoned. When you drink this water you will die from it, they said, then when you read this book, you will die from that. They led you into forests, they stuck you inside gloomy nurseries in order to destroy you, and they introduced you to people whom you immediately realized would be your destroyers. They showed you landscapes which would be fatal for you. They tossed you into schools as though into dungeons; ultimately, they drove your soul from you to let it perish in their swamp and in their desert. In this way, early on, they gave your heart its compliant rhythm until it became, as the doctors say, terminally ill because they gave you this heart of yours which never rests.

They stuffed you into green clothes when you wanted to wear red ones in the cold, when warm ones were needed, if you wanted to walk, you had to run, if you wanted to run, you had to walk, if you wanted rest, they gave you none, if you wanted to cry, they plugged your mouth. You have always observed them for as long you can remember and seen their hypocrisy and studied them and told them over and over again that they were doomed, something they refused to believe even though they knew they were nothing but doomed the whole time they had been under my observation down to the present. What they have always denied is that they are shameless, unscrupulous, dangerous. Then they accused me of telling the truth, so to speak. But when I occasionally said that they are good-looking, intelligent, so as to tell the truth, they accused me of lying. Thus have they accused me all my life of the truth sometimes and of lying sometimes and of the truth and of lying quite frequently, but essentially they have accused me of the truth and of lying all my life, just as I have accused them of lying and the truth all their lives.

I can say whatever I want, and they will accuse me of either the truth or of lying and it is not clear if they accuse me now of the truth or of lying, as I am not so often clear when I accuse them of lying or of the truth, since I, inside my mechanism of accusation, which has already turned into my disease of accusation, can no longer tell whether it is the truth or a lie, just as they can no longer tell a lie apart from truth to me. Earlier I was in a state of mortal terror taking a lump of sugar from the dining room tin, that is why I am in mortal fear today taking a book from the library, and I am in the greatest mortal fear if it's a philosophical one like yesterday evening. I have always loved Montaigne like no other. I have always escaped to my Montaigne when I felt mortal fear. With Montaigne I conduct and control myself, and, yes, lead and mislead as well. Montaigne has always been my saviour and redeemer. When I mistrust everyone else ultimately in my infinitely large philosophical family, which I can only describe as an infinitely large French philosophical family, where there are a few German and Italian nephews and nieces, but who have all, I must admit, died rather prematurely, I have always been in good hands with my Montaigne.

I have never had a father and never a mother but I have always had Montaigne. My begetters, whom I will never call father and mother, rejected me from the very first moment and, early on, I drew the consequences from this rejection and ran straight away into the arms of my Montaigne, which is the truth. Montaigne, I have always thought, had an infinitely large philosophical family, but I have never loved any of these philosophical family members as much as their head, my Montaigne.

On the way into the tower, in the library, and in the darkness because of the mosquitoes, I wanted to cling to some member of this French philosophical family after I had freed myself from the clutches of my own, but at no time did I think that even in the greatest darkness I had in hand, securely gripped, my Montaigne. My family ate their soup and meat with like rapaciousness, something I always found odious about them, how they put spoon to mouth, something which says more about them than anything else; how they slice meat on the serving tray, take salad from the bowl. How they drink from their glasses and pull apart the bread and, not to mention, the way they talk about something and fight over of it or make fun of it has always been odious and embarrassing to me. I have always taken my meals with them, but I have been forced to do so all my life, to be together with them, to be at their mercy because of my illness.

Most of the time, to say not more than a hundred steps without them would be unsettling if such an expression did not fill me with horror. Everything about them and involving them (and involving me) would be unsettling to say if such an expression did not fill me with horror as nothing else can. First they had made me dependent on them, then they accused me of being dependent on them for my entire life. From that time on, when I could no longer get out of being dependent on them, it was my natural state, my excruciatingly natural state. From a certain point in time I had to tell myself the only way there is is with them.

We want to escape, to flee, but we can't any more. They (and we ourselves) have bricked up all the exits to the open air. Suddenly, we see that they (like us) have walled us inside. Then we wait only for the moment when we choke to death. Then we often think whether it wouldn't be better to be blind, perfectly deaf to our other crippling diseases, which we have to recognize as fatal because then we will see nothing more, hear nothing more, but at once that becomes self-deception too. We always wanted to be healed when no cure was expected because one was no longer possible. We always wanted to break out where there was no more breaking out.

My family had been too late in seeing that they had bred their destroyer and annihilator. And I understood too late. I understood when it was too late to know to

understand. How often they said they would have preferred a dog to me, because a dog would have guarded
them and cost less than me, who only watches and scorns
them and subverts and destroys and annihilates.

If you go to the well, we will beat you to death, they
said when I was four or five years old. If you go into the
library, you will see, they said, and meant nothing less than
I would be beaten for it. Thus I am forever like this four-
or five-year-old child secretly at the well and like this
grown-up, so to speak, always secretly going into the
library. Thus did they always give me to understand that
I would acquire this so-called excess baggage at the well
and fall irretrievably down. And they always gave me to
understand that in the library and in very specific, but
without directly saying, philosophical books, I would
acquire this excess baggage and fall irretrievably down.
How I went secretly into the library from the age of four
or five, until my soul froze inside, going into the library
for so many years in secret, behind their backs, so to speak.

Each time it seems as though I have entered a trap,
because they have always told me or gave me to understand that the library is a trap for me (like the well). I am
forty-two years old and enter the library like a trap. The
trap will snap shut, they said, as I entered the library for
the first time. Each time, when I enter the library, I think
the trap snaps shut. It could also be Descartes, I thought,
Pascal too. My God, I thought, how I love all these

philosophers as I love nothing else in the world! But it was Montaigne, my beloved above all Montaigne! I sat in the deepest recess of the tower and read and read and might have cried out for joy had I not long ago repressed such a grotesque display of wonderfully letting go with this thought: When we cry out irrepressibly and don't see ourselves as a result and don't regard ourselves at this opportunity, we are even more ludicrous than we have already made ourselves out to be, thus I saw myself as though I had cried out and regarded this truth without really and actually crying out.

I read from my Montaigne by the fastened shutters in this most absurd way, for it is very hard without artificial light, up until this sentence: Hopefully nothing happened to him! That sentence was not from Montaigne, but from my family, who searched for me under the tower, back and forth.

Reunion

While I always expressed myself too *loudly*, and especially the word *misery* always too loudly, I said it was invariably typical of him to invariably say everything too softly, something that made it difficult throughout our time together, especially when we so often went walking in the forest every day, as it had been our custom towards the end of winter, speaking not a word to each other in self-evident consent, as I said emphatically, without hesitation; we had become accustomed to the rhythm of our walking, I said, the rhythm of our feelings and thoughts, although I was more in keeping with *my* feelings and thoughts than to his, and from this rhythm of walking one developed this entirely appropriate rhythm of speech, especially in the High Alps, where we had so often gone with our parents, who went twice a year to the mountains and always made us go with them to the mountains, even though we hated the mountains. He hated the mountains just as much as I did and, from the beginning of our relationship, our hatred of the mountains was just the means that brought us close for the first time and finally bound us together for years and decades. Even the arrangements of our parents for the mountains made us turn against them and furious with the mountains, with the fresh air, and with our parents' unalleviated, long-awaited *peace and quiet*, which they believed they could find in the mountains and only in the mountains, but never did they find it in themselves, as we knew; even when they spoke of their latest impending Alpine holiday, when they packed their Alpine paraphernalia and confronted us with this packing of their Alpine paraphernalia, it made us furious with their Alpine intentions and with their Alpine passion and ultimately with their Alpine madness, and we were as much repelled by their Alpine intentions and passion as we were by their Alpine madness. Your parents had a much greater Alpine passion than mine, I said, and I said it again too loudly for him, which is probably why I didn't get his answer, so with that I said his parents always had bright green wool stockings, not like mine, ones of bright red, that his pulled on these bright green stockings so as not to at all stand out in their seeking nature, while mine pulled on bright red so as to stand out in nature, his parents had always spared nothing in asserting their intention to not stand out in nature, while mine had always spared nothing to stand out in this nature, his parents had always said they wore bright green stockings in order not to stand out in nature, my parents had always said they wore bright red

in order to stand out in nature, and his justified their bright
green stockings with the same tenacity as mine did their
bright red. And then at every moment they made a point
of how they had knitted those bright green and bright red
stockings themselves, *your* mother I always saw knitting
those bright green stockings, I said, *mine* the bright red as
though she had nothing other on her mind, I said, when
it grew dark, than knitting those bright red ones and yours
those bright green. And your parents always had on bright
green caps in their bright green stockings, I said, mine
bright red. Indeed, in the High Alps, accident victims will
more easily be found wearing bright red stockings and
bright red caps than other ones, I said to him, but he
didn't answer. His parents had always treated me with suspicion, I said, always letting me into their house with suspicion and it was always unnerving for me to visit his
parents' house given this suspicion, but my parents were
always just as much suspicious of him, and so his parents
very often prevented me from coming to see him, and
mine did the same when he came to see me, when I
wanted nothing more deeply than his coming to see me,
for I had long felt throughout my childhood and long
afterwards that he was my liberator from the prison house
of my parents that I had always found deadly. I know too
that his parents treated him the same way, that his house
was just as much a prison. Not for nothing did we mutu-
ally agree to always call our childhood homes *that grey
house*. For as long as we lived in our childhood homes, we

were incarcerated in two prison cells, and if one of us believed that he had been locked up in a terrible prison, the other in short order schooled him of one far worse, letting him know whose prison was more terrible. Our childhood homes are always prisons and very few break out, I said to him, at most, and that means about 98 per cent, I would think, remain locked up in this prison for their entire lives, getting slammed into this prison and ultimately ruined and in truth dying in this prison. But I broke out, I said to him, I broke out of that prison at sixteen and have been free ever since. His parents always showed me how *cruel* parents can be, as mine showed him in kind how awful parents are. When we met between our parents' houses, on the bench beneath the yew tree, I said, Do you remember how we talked about our parents' prisons and how it is possible to break free of them, that we had come up with plans, but just as quickly gave them up because it was utterly hopeless, that we had talked again and again of the harshening of a disciplinary machine for which we had no recourse. My parents always reproached me for just being there, I said to him, in the same way as yours always reproached you, and for that reason they punished me, they continually referred to me as *the* intruder who prevented and ultimately destroyed their marital and thus their human development, as yours always said to you, that you destroyed theirs, I said. When you came home, they welcomed you with only threats, as mine did me when I came home, I was always received with some threat, especially that fatal one, that I would be their death. We were incapable of knowing how they had willingly made us, I said, and when I knew, it was too late to use that in my defence. My parents little by little put me into solitary confinement, I said, as yours little by little put you into solitary confinement. And the air holes, which we had in the beginning, they bricked up little by little. Finally, we had no more air, I said. The walls, which they had erected around us, always became thicker, soon we no longer heard anything, as nothing more of the outside world penetrated our thick walls. Your mother had always worn her hair loose, I said, mine always tight and smooth on her head. Over time she talked on and on to me evermore incomprehensibly, with absolute incomprehensibleness, I said to him, but when I said that I didn't understand her, she punished me. My relationship with her was such a machine of punishment that over time I could only assume this cowering position around her. Like you, I said, who also had to approach your mother cowering, continually in fear of coming by a blow on the head or an unspeakable word. On Sundays, which were always said to be a day of peace, we had hell at home, I said. Waking up was nothing more than looking into hell, I said, when I washed myself, I was afraid that I would do it wrong, and so the bar of soap frequently slipped from me, I said, and I crawled on the floor to find it, my whole body shaking, you know. I could barely comb myself, for I couldn't relax. When I dressed I continually feared that my mother might come in and slap my face for a reason I wouldn't know, for having carelessly pulled my belt around my waist too tight or too loose, or because a button was missing on my shirt, or because of a ruined crease in my trousers or for being stained with tears. At breakfast I already looked utterly given up on life, like a person nearly destroyed, sitting at the table as the family's shame. And no matter what, they made it immediately clear to me that I was the family's shame, why did they even give me a name, I often thought, when from the very start they could have just called me the family's shame, which I always was and always would be. And when I think back, I said to him, I see that it wasn't any different for you either, perhaps you only spoke of it less than I did, I said, always less than I spoke of it, but you always went through the same thing, I said, it was always the same way for you, for both of us, whatever affected you likewise affected me. That silence with which my mother always mistreated me, I said, which always deeply wounded my soul. That silence was my mother's means of inflicting me with a fatal wound. My father had been the silent partner in this atrocity, the spectator to my destruction by my mother. And when I think back, it had been likewise with your mother and with your father. They had a good life, I said, but they only existed by destroying me. And over time, while they destroyed you, your parents lived quite well in their home, which had only been a prison for you, from which you haven't left your whole life, for unlike me, who broke out, you are never going to break out because you no longer have the strength for it. Then they filled their backpacks, I said, and gloated on the contempt I showed for them on such occasions. I hated everything they stuffed in those backpacks, the spare pairs of stockings, the spare hats, as I said, the sausage, the bread, the butter, the cheese, the bandages, etcetera. In the end my father always packed a Bible that he would read in the cabin. Always the same passages with always the same tone, you remember. And we had to listen and could not say a thing. We were not allowed to say a thing the entire time during our Alpine holidays. When we said something, it was considered insolence and inevitably led to being punished. If that were the case, given the circumstances we had to go uphill faster, downhill quicker, since our offensive or rather criminal words were so enormous, to protest how heinous it was to drink nothing when we were thirsty, to eat nothing when we were hungry. I came to feel my mother's harshness on these Alpine holidays especially, her implacability. Father was invariably just a spectator to her harshness and implacability, not once as I recall, did my father interrupt his spectating with a comment for or against her, never mind any objection. Mother was the cruel one, father was the spectator to this cruelty, I said, and your parents were likewise. Your father too said nothing as your mother tormented you with her nagging and nearly beat you to death with her canings. Fathers let mothers do as they please with their mania for destruction and don't lift a finger. We were killed by our parents, I said. But with you everything had been much worse than with me, for I really did break out, freed myself, while you never freed yourself, and while you did indeed separate from your parents, who are your breeders and whelpers and tormentors, you didn't really free yourself of them. At sixteen it's almost too late, I said, because then you just go through the world that points a finger at you, a person still destroyed, for even at a distance he is plainly a person destroyed. The world is ruthless when it sees such a person destroyed by his parents, I said. I walked away from them and wanted to get as far as possible, but I soon fell apart, I said. We both wanted to break out, I said, but I had the strength, you didn't. Your parents' prison turned out to be lifelong for you. So you sat apathetically in your room, I said, and stared at the paintings they hung in your room, these valuable but nevertheless fatal pictures. You had locked yourself in this room and only walked around and around with chains on your feet, from one feeding to the next in the end, which is the truth: decades. You arranged things with your wardens. They taught you what books to read, what pictures to look at, what music to listen to. They taught you how to call into the forest until the corresponding echo returned and you didn't resist. For decades now you stare at pictures in this way, as your parents instructed you, with this mindless look, and you read books with the same mindlessness and mindlessly listen to music too the way your parents taught you. You say the same thing   about Goya that your parents continuously said about Goya, you read Goethe the same way as your parents and you listen to Mozart like them, in the most vulgar way. But I made myself independent, because I took the opportunity at the decisive moment, I said, and freed myself and listened to Mozart this way, as *I* hear him, contrary to my parents, thus contrary to my exterminators, I see Goya this way, as *I* see him, contrary to my parental exterminators, I read Goethe, if I read him at all, this way, as *I* read him. Then they always, as the last thing, fastened the zither and trumpet to their backpacks, before they left the house, as is proper for musical people. My mother always said this *as is proper for musical people*, it followed me to my bed the whole night and I couldn't shut it out. She played the zither because her mother played the same zither, father played the trumpet because his father played the same trumpet. And because his father had always sketched when he was in the High Alps, my father, too, always sketched in the High Alps and he always had a sketchpad in his backpack. *Like Segantini*, he always said, *like Hodler, like Waldmüller*. He picked out a pinnacle rock and sat upon it like so, with the sun at his back, and sketched. Eventually we had every room in our house filled with his drawings, nowhere was there a blank spot, for he had hundreds, if not thousands of Alpine landscapes in the house, and in order to not see them I had to direct my eyes continuously at the floor, but over time that drove me mad, I said. He drew the Ortler or painted it in watercolours a hundred times, the Drei Zinnen a hundred times and Mont Blanc and the Matterhorn over and over again. *The great masters*, he always said, *always painted or sketched the same thing. They are only great because they always painted and sketched the same thing.* But what my father painted was disgusting, I said. The talent of his father, my grandfather, had utterly atrophied in him, but that didn't prevent him from degenerating into this monstrous production of drawings and watercolours. The abomination surely was, I said, that so many cultural associations mounted exhibitions with his productions and the newspapers wrote only good things about his drawings and watercolours and that spurred him on to ever-greater output. And the people of his milieu really were of the opinion that he was an artist, many had said so over and over again that he was a great artist, such that eventually even he believed that nonsense and that vulgarity and persisted in that ghastly delusion. When demonstrating what is kitsch, I said, merely submit a few of my father's drawings or watercolours. *My house is a permanent exhibition of my art*, said my father and every few weeks he pinned or taped another drawing or watercolour on the walls, I said, and in the cellar he had accumulated thousands. I am the High Alps specialist, he said of himself, *I have surpassed Segantini, surpassed Hodler, whose art I have long since left behind*. He even hung as many drawings in the kitchen as was possible in the belief that the air of cooking had the direct effect of perfecting his works. If I let the air of cooking act on my work for a few weeks, he said, especially during the winter months and especially over the Christmas holiday, these sheets will acquire an enormous charm. Then he collected stones, I said, do you remember. There was nothing to object to about it, I guess, for all these stones were quite strange looking and he lugged them home himself. They lie there to this day by the thousands. In such large numbers, they are so strange, unbearable, I said. An entire row of these stones have the form of human bodies, I said, mostly female, and he found them in Swiss rills for the most part, in the Engadin. When it comes to one of those particular stones, he always said, it isn't possible to determine if it's really a stone polished by millions of years or an early work of art, *nature isn't capable of producing such breasts*, he said over and over again holding the stone up to light, *such an inspired head*. I remember, I said, that my father once showed this stone to you as well. *This is a statue, he exclaimed, thousands of years old, no product of nature, a work of art.* They always locked up everything, I said, your parents, and mine too, while I wanted everything left open, I hate doors which are locked, wherever I am, I always leave my door unlocked. And they always cleaned everything up, hardly had I set down some object and they cleared it away again, in this way they totally and systematically suppressed any human development in our house, I said, they always had this fear that our house could suddenly spring to life through my sister and myself. They caught on to anything personal, if not from the outset, then in the shortest time, thus did we feel our house as a morgue. The word *discipline*, which was often spoken in our house, prevented any development. When I came back home, everything was as it had been again when I woke up, I said to him. That morgue, as my sister and I always described our house, was reconstituted. *No one will stand out*, my mother often said and cleared away any articles of clothing, shoes, et cetera, which had been taken off in the house. I said: Do you remember the heavy shoes they squeezed us in? The heavy hats they put on us? The heavy Loden capes they pulled over us? The blinds were closed all year on three sides of the house, I said, only there, where it had been important for my father's drawings and watercolours, were they left open. And they always closed every one of them in your house, I said, summer and winter, as was said, in summer for the mosquitoes and flies, in winter for the cold and for your mother's neuritis, do you remember? So you had this pale complexion all year long, as though you were deathly ill, I said. Only when we went with our parents up to the High Alps did our faces get any colour, but not tan, like our parents' faces, but red. In contrast to our parents' tan faces, our faces turned red in no time at all and our lips blistered, and for weeks we couldn't sleep because of our sunburn. This is the reason why we were hated by our parents, because we were incapable of getting the uniform tan complexions as they did in the High Alps but, rather, swollen red complexions. And for months afterwards our

eyes suffered from that appalling Alpine sunlight, such that
we couldn't read for a long time, do you remember? Our
eyes ached and we fell behind in school because of those
aching eyes, as these Alpine holidays with our parents
always had a devastating effect on us. Essentially, everything about our parents was rough, they were rough and
ruthless to us our whole lives, I said, whenever they should
have always been circumspect with us, caring. Mother
slammed the doors behind her all the time, Father tram-
pled through the house in his old climbing boots. Twice
during the year they went into the mountains to find
peace and quiet, but of course they only brought wherever they went their lack of peace and quiet, and of course
the valleys in which they went really did have peace and
quiet, but only as long as they did not enter them, the
forests peace and quiet as long as they didn't walk in them,
the summits of mountains as long as they weren't climbing
them. The mountain cabins which they frequented naturally had peace and quiet as long as my parents did not
frequent them, I said. Ultimately, the most peaceful and
quiet place was also our homes when our parents were
away, naturally, I said. People like our parents never find
peace and quiet, I said, because they themselves *are* the
absence of peace and quiet, and this absence of peace and
quiet is everywhere they are and everywhere they go.
They seek peace and quiet, but they never find it, naturally, because they are the absence of peace and quiet, they
set out to find a restful place and by their very appearance

transform a restful place into a restless one, the most restful into the most restless. But here is peace and quiet, they say, and look around themselves, and it is in truth an unquiet place because they have stepped in it. It was absurd when Father said, I will have my peace and quiet. Just like it was when Mother said it. And when I said it, too, finally, because all three of us were the absence of peace and quiet, the parents as far back as I can think, me because of my parents. My parents made me restless and I will no more find peace and quiet, I said, as you too find no more peace and quiet because your parents made you restless. Because a human being, in his original state, is this peace and quiet, I said, and he will only be made into someone restless by his parents through the parental system which has ultimately become the world system for every individual. Thus there exists in nature no relaxed human beings, I said, all of them are restless and when they seek peace and quiet, it is a form of madness. Sooner or later everyone falls into this folly of seeking peace and quiet when peace and quiet don't exist because a human being is the absence of peace and quiet, and wherever he goes this absence of peace and quiet exists, and wherever he isn't, he won't find it. When we look for peace and quiet, it's the greatest folly, I said. All of us are looking for peace and quiet round the clock and, of course, we don't find it because we are the absence of peace and quiet ourselves. These Alpine holidays were undertaken twice a year in error by my parents, for they could find no peace and quiet in the High Alps. In the mountain cabin. On the mountaintop. On the contrary, these Alpine holidays intensified the absence of peace and quiet in all of us. When we think we have come into peace and quiet, we are at our most restless, I said, you understand. Of course, my parents didn't understand, for they were suspicious of thinking all their lives. They would find fault, but they would not think, they confused *finding fault* with *thinking* and there are almost as many fault-finders in the world as there are people, but hardly any thinkers. That fallacy of finding peace and quiet was surely one of many that my parents had cultivated, I said. They pulled on their bright red stockings and put on their bright red caps and went on this search for peace and quiet. They always assumed there would be peace and quiet in the High Alps, in Switzerland or the South Tyrol, near Merano, in the vicinity the Seiser Alm, on the Ortler, on Mont Blanc, in the vicinity of the Matterhorn or the Toten Gebirge. They pulled on their bright red stockings and put on their bright red hats and fastened a zither and trumpet to their backpacks and walked in peace and quiet. But they did not find it. And in the end, I said, they put the blame on *me* for having not found it. *I* was the obstacle, the original sin for everything. Me and my sister, we were the ones who destroyed their plans. For months, when they tossed the sentence *I will have my peace and quiet* at each other's heads, packed their backpacks, went on that quest for peace and quiet. They purchased the requisite train tickets and travelled in the direction of peace and quiet. They were each certain that they would find peace and quiet in a valley in Switzerland or on a mountain crest or on a peak in the South Tyrol. Going ever faster, climbing ever higher. At last, using pick and rope, zither and trumpet. But they didn't find peace and quiet. At first they always believed it to be something easy, to find peace and quiet, but then they saw that it was the hardest of things. In their failure to find peace and quiet, they began to accuse me. Hesitantly at first, they were plagued by scruples in the hotel dining room, along the timberline, and then suddenly, on the verge of exhaustion and in the realization of total failure, they fell upon me, the original sinner, the original misfortune, the one who allowed them *not once in the mountains* peace and quiet. And your parents, I said, used the same approach on you. The sole reason my parents always took me along into the High Alps was to make me responsible for their failure in this search for rest, just as they always regarded me as responsible for every kind of hardship and horror. They always turned on me, when they had to unload their hate for everything on me, me, standing there at their disposal. Thus, even with them on the highest mountain peak, I said, I had to be standing at their disposal for their fatal intentions, which they didn't shrink from, beating and kicking me up the Ortler in order to accuse me of their unhappiness atop the summit. And your parents did the same to you, I said. Your father released his anger on you, just as we reached the foot of the Glockner Glacier, dead tired, I said, wiped out. Do you remember? The storm rose and I was to blame, the avalanche fell and they said I had set it off. The peak of our parents' hate for us was also on that mountain's summit, I said, for their failed productions, as my mother often said, for *the disgrace. I will have my peace and quiet*, my father said and packed his climbing boots and his sketchpad, and mother packed her backpack and tuned her zither in the kitchen because it seemed the best place to her, and they abused me, since I packed my things too slowly along with a disgusting book as well, the Novalis poems as I remember, and we dashed to the railroad station and departed into the darkness so that we could start climbing at first light. Before we even got up, I was already exhausted, and you were already exhausted, I said, not to mention my sister. Silently, without protest, we had to go. Until my father got ahead of the group, for he was the most robust, always getting further ahead, and ultimately being the first to begin the ascent as well. My mother was only bitter. My sister wailed, nothing helped. Father decided the route. Mother followed him without a word, and I distinctly remember the sound of the strings on her zither hanging from her backpack. *I will have my peace and quiet*, this sentence, although no one said it, was continually said, this sentence was not produced in my head, I heard over and over, that *I will have my peace and quiet* of my father. He raced ahead of us with his giant strides so as to be in keeping with his sentence *I will have my peace and quiet*, but when the sentence could not be kept up with, he pressed on again and again. He was there too as we neared the summit, and he was still there when we were already atop the summit exhausted and looking down into the landscape below us. Never have I seen the world more threatening and dangerous than from the summit of a mountain. While my father said a number of times, *what peace and quiet reigns on top of the summit, a majestic peace and quiet*, he said, for he could no longer tolerate the loud absence of peace and quiet, for the absence of peace and quiet is there, where you would expect peace and quiet to be at their greatest and absolute, to be at their greatest of all and at the most absolute, and he tormented himself time and again with this remark that now he was in the greatest peace and quiet, we were suddenly in the greatest peace and quiet, he said, and he said to us, as though we didn't hear, that we were in this greatest and utterly absolute peace and quiet, he continually demanded, I said, that my mother say and admit that we were now in this greatest and absolute peace and quiet and mother too said a couple of times that we were in this greatest and absolute peace and quiet, *how still, how quiet it is here, everything is peaceful*, she said, *the greatest peace and quiet of all is here.* And since I was never of the same mind as my parents, I said, they requested that I say up here on the summit reigned absolute peace and quiet and so I, to put an end to their threats, also said that up here on the summit reigned the greatest peace and quiet, absolute peace and quiet. If I had not said that, if I had told the truth, namely, that the greatest absence of peace and quiet, that absolute absence of peace and quiet was on top of this mountain summit, they would have really hurt me, I said. Thus they contented themselves while I said several times the words *greatest and absolute peace and quiet*. Then as we sat huddled inside a wind-protected crevice, my mother eventually undid the zither from her backpack and started to play. She always played the zither badly, unlike my grandmother who could play like no one else, and on the summit her playing had been a catastrophe that time, I said. Father shouted at her to stop playing the zither, I said, whereupon he undid the trumpet from his backpack and played it. But the wind played havoc with his trumpet notes and soon spoilt it for him. He inserted his trumpet between two slabs of rock and let Mother cut him two large pieces of bread on which he put several slices of ham. They also gave me something to eat, but I could not get down a single bite, as they say. *Such peace and quiet*, my father said several times. The wind soon became a storm, I said, and we were certain that we would freeze to death on the spot. So we huddled inside the rock shelter and stared out. The storm is a good sign, my father said. Yes, said my mother, I said. And the way up had taken eight hours. My parents pressed themselves together in the crevice and their bodies shook. The storm was so loud that I could hardly understand as Father said: *What peace and quiet reigns here*. He too was exhausted, like Mother.

As to me, I only know that I didn't know how I was able to follow my parents. They pulled off their climbing boots and stretched their legs and feet and rubbed each other's toes. For me it was like I was dreaming, I said. From that time on I hated the Ortler, I said. But every couple of years it had to be the Ortler, I said, I don't know why. And your parents, every two years at least, took you up the Ortler as well. And then you were exhausted for months and laid low, do you remember? I said. Surely my parents never went off by themselves with a book in order to read it as they always claimed, I said, it was always just a pretext in order to deprive us. As your parents did to you. *Leave us in peace*! really had but one purpose, to be able to fight without witnesses, to wear one down, as my mother so aptly characterized it. Father sought peace and quiet in his room in order to be in an even greater absence of peace and quiet in his room, as Mother did in hers. If Father went into the garden to have peace and quiet, he worked digging and working the soil and trimming trees ever deeper into his absence of peace and quiet, so too when he went into the city, just like wherever he went, I said. And it was the same way with Mother, who continuously wanted peace and quiet and only ended up in deeper agitation until she began to pack her backpack, for she saw that Father had already packed his. Then it was only a question of where, Switzerland or the South Tyrol. In Switzerland they travelled full of themselves, to the South Tyrol out of hypocrisy, a vile sentimentality. Your parents always travelled with my parents and climbed the mountains, I said, yours always along with mine, never the other way round, and we had to come along and climb along. And instead of being rested, our parents always came back from the Swiss and South Tyrolese mountains exhausted, we ourselves more or less insane, I said, deathly ill. My sister was affected the most, I said, because she was always the most vulnerable of us all, the one who could never have resisted in the slightest. That she died at twenty-one was entirely consistent, I said, her parents killed her, and she could not, as I did, escape their murderous intentions. Parents make a child and strive above all else to destroy it, I said, my parents just like yours and every parent altogether and everywhere. Parents afford the luxury of children and kill them. And they all have their assorted, equivalent methods. Our parents destroyed us while all the time holding it against us that we were to blame for their lack of peace and quiet and ultimately for everything concerning them. For our parents, the shoe fit us for *everything blameworthy*, this is the truth. So, the suspicion cannot be rejected out of hand, I said, of whether our parents made us for no other reason than to personify their guilt, I said, it is possible that we have been nothing but the impersonators of their guilt for our entire lives and remain so as the ones held accountable for them. Our parents made us for the sole purpose of dumping their guilt, so that they could make the shoe fit us, I said. If Father had been irritated, I was the cause, if Mother was agitated, I had caused her agitation. If the air was bad in the house, I was to blame. If the front door had not been locked at night, it was me even though I knew that it could not have been me. *At last you have peace and quiet*! my father often called to me and my sister, and then he took us to the mountains instead of going alone, most likely for the one and only reason, so that he could dump all the guilt on us once more. If we arrived too late at the guesthouse or the cabin, we were to blame, do you remember? I said, if the bread got wet in the backpack, I was to blame. And such were thousands of examples for this relationship, I said, this terrible one that existed between me and us and so between my sister and me towards my parents. If my father was bothered by mosquitoes during the night, he thereupon accused me of being in his room and of having turned the light on with the windows open, something that was not only strictly forbidden but also should have been self-evident. And just as yours did, mine always called me a hypochondriac when it came to my illnesses, a charlatan when it came to my reading regimen, to my later writing, do you remember? I said. So much is clear, I said, that was completely out of mind for decades. Just this awfulness and atrociousness, I said, something a man dare not say any more, since his perpetrators are long dead. But all at once I dare to tell myself of all this awfulness and appallingness. It is even easy for me. It can't be appalling and awful enough. When we came back from the High Alps I was properly punished for my *behaviour in the High Alps*. Like you too, I said. I remember in detail. Then they reproached me for my rotten behaviour in Switzerland, in Engadin or the South Tyrol, atop the Ortler, enumerating everything for me and contriving a perfidious penal system. They reproached me for having not looked far or long enough at the beautiful scenery, for defying their commands, for sleeping during the day and not at night, as is proper, as my father often said. I had a wrong relationship with nature, no eye for the grandeur of creation, no ear for the songs of birds, for the roaring of the streams, for the rushing of the wind, and this horrendous eye for nothing. Then they reduced the times I could eat and deliberately removed my favourite foods from the planning of meals. I could no longer go out for weeks and had to wear only the clothes which I hated. And for you it fared just the same when your parents came back from the High Alps, I said. Father spread out his drawings and watercolours in his room and I had to say to every one of these drawings and watercolours what they represented and that they were the best. If I made a mistake, unable to remember the so-called *natural models* despite my best attempts, he became angry. Your father read you poems which he had composed on those Alpine trips, I said, and you either didn't listen or you listened but could find nothing to say about those poems, I said, for which you would be punished by your father. Your father had published three books of poems, I said, my father held as many exhibitions of his drawings and watercolours, in this way our fathers believed they were escaping by only attempting the trite, so to speak, wanting from this *walking fanatic art* to redeem themselves in a roundabout way, something which didn't pan out. Instead, they debased themselves in these drawings and watercolours and with these poems, published at that. They insisted on their debasement in this way, I said, and insist on it even though they are long dead, even now. If my father didn't succeed in a drawing, he blamed me, for I had been standing in the light, I said, by talking to him I had destroyed his intuition, as he always put it. I was always just the destroyer of his artistic world. *The son exists in this world only to be the destroyer of the artist who is his father*, my father once said, do you remember? I said. He painted worse than he drew, I said, the same way my mother played the zither, so he painted and drew, if anything, even worse, but he spoke all the time about his artistry, of even being from an artistic family, meaning ours. The same way your father called himself a poet, I said, even though his poetry didn't merit this designation at all, for it was just rhymed imbecility, as you know. Bound and put on sale made them much more vulgar than at home on his desk, I said. And for as long as my father lived, I wrote not one line, I said. Only when he was dead did I attempt to write a sketch about his dead face, I said. This sketch turned out well to me. But then I did nothing more for years. All nonsense, insipid, irrelevant, worthless. And only when your father was dead did you leave home, I said, turning your back on your mother, so to speak, was the high point of your life. You deprived yourself of her, but you still suffered over this. I have never suffered over leaving my parents behind me, I had been under them for so long, fatally damaged, I said, I never had a reason to feel remorse for them as you did for your parents. That's the difference, I said. Because I broke out of prison and you didn't. Because I turned my back at six-teen and you only as an old man. That is the truth. At fifty-two you are nothing but an old man. Embittered, nothing else. The world has left you behind, I said, passed you by. You are unsightly, I said. You still have on your father's coat, as I can see, and not only the real one, this threadbare and shabby one, forty years old, but also this other one, the so-called spiritual mantle of the father. You are stuck in this mantle of the father. Under the eyes of your mother, who had said nothing moreover, I said. The one who always watched, giving it her all to watch to the last degree as you went to seed in the mantle of the father. For you are a dissolute human being, of that there is no doubt, I said. But probably you, unlike me, never had the chance to break away, to turn your back on your parents, you had to wait for your father's death, so that your eyes opened to your mother too, that she had been your destroyer too, just as much as your father. What you've told me about their suffering simply repels me, I said. False sentimentality always repels me and you always speak of them with this false sentimentality. You have never broken from the false and hypo-critical sentimentality of your parents' house. Everything that you say is false and hypo-critical, you crouch with falsehood and hypocrisy in your father's coat, I said. I have never put on a stitch of my father's clothing, never, you wear your father's shabby coat at fifty-two. That had to make you realize at long last that a man should never slip on the clothes of his parents. But you just put on father's coat and draw yourself up tight inside it. Your mewling is nauseating, I said. I am sick of childhood. Especially that mewling that has to do with childhood, that mewling brought before the court of life time and time again. All of this is repugnant, I said. To think of these parents is nothing but repugnant. These people had no right to find peace and quiet at all, I said. And for their entire lives they never found peace and quiet either, I said. *I will have my peace and quiet*, as put by my father (and yours too) was nothing more than perverse. I am convinced, I said, when you are alone in your house, the one still your parents' house, perhaps during the hours of twilight, that you pull on your father's bright green stockings and, while sitting on the edge of your bed, imagine that you are now climbing the Matterhorn. And you have a bright green cap on your head too, which your mother knitted, she knitted dozens of such bright green caps, just as mine knitted dozens of bright red ones. The bright red because they are seen in case of an accident, if I'm not right, I said, the bright green for its wearers to remain inconspicuous. What an absurdity, I said, you sit on the edge of your bed with your tongue hanging out, I said, and you have on bright green Alpine stockings and the bright green Alpine cap and you imagine yourself climbing up the Matterhorn, or even more exquisite, I said, up the Ortler. You play with the Matterhorn in your way, I said, with the Ortler, and possibly with your mother playing along. I can picture your mother going into raptures as a result. And on the summit you two face off, screaming nothing but accusations at each other. You are from the family of the bright green stockings and bright green caps, I said, I from the family of bright red. After my parents were dead, I found in a box and in two chests of drawers nothing but hundreds of bright red Alpine caps, I said, nothing but bright red Alpine stockings. Every one of them knitted by my mother. My parents could have gone into the High Alps with these bright red caps and bright red stockings for thousands of years. I burnt every one of those bright red caps and bright red stockings, I said. I put on one of my mother's hundreds of bright red Alpine caps and in this costume burnt all the others, laughing, laughing, continuously laughing, I said. Most likely your mother knitted just as many bright green caps and bright green stockings as mine did, however, you don't have the courage to find them, you only need to open one or another drawer in your house, and then they will spring at you by the hundreds, I said. For decades our mothers knitted these caps and stockings. You do remember that they always knitted these caps and stockings, I said, you do remember? I always saw your mother knitting such bright green stockings and bright green caps when I had been to your house, I said, these hats and stockings have to be somewhere still. Hundreds of bright green caps and bright green stockings, I said, in the course of life. I always saw your mother knitting these bright green caps and bright green stockings. Don't you remember, I asked. To that he said that he didn't remember. He took the six o'clock train and had missed his connection here at the station in Schwarzach–Sankt Veit. He was completely soaked, he said and I just looked at him and saw that he was completely soaked. We haven't seen each other in twenty years, I said, and how you said the word *misery* is still clear in my head, I said. And that I always spoke louder than you. We haven't spoken much, but I've always spoken louder than you, I said. I said he ought to get up and go inside the restaurant with me where it is surely warm. No, he said, he didn't want that, he would sit on the bench until his train arrived. I said that I wouldn't have recognized him had it not been for his father's coat, which I knew well. Do you remember how we stayed in Flims? I asked him. He shook his head. Don't you remember, I asked. No, he said, and then with a very quiet and very weak voice: *I remember nothing whatsoever.*

Going Up in Flames:

A Travelogue to an Erstwhile Friend

As you know I have been on the run over four months now, not in a southerly direction as I suggested to you but rather a northerly one, since warmth did not attract me as it turned out, but rather cold, not the *architecture*, my dear architect and building artist but rather *nature* and specifically *northern nature* as a matter of fact, of which you have so often spoken, the so-called *Arctic Circle nature*, about which I have already drafted a work thirty years ago, one of my countless secret works, cryptograms, never intended for publication, for I recently had this intention of going on living again, not only to prolong my existence, but I want to carry on with this absolute lack of restraint as well, my dear architect, my dear building artist, my dear surface-area charlatan. Secretly epoch-making, so to speak, in collusion, my dear sir. At first I thought I would never write to you again under any circumstances, because our relationship certainly appears to have come to a de facto and irreversible end to me for many years now, especially to its intellectual end, my intention naturally being to never again have any further contact with you, to write not a single line any more, because any line more seemed to me utter nonsense after such a long time, addressed to a person, to a friend once for decades, who once had been an intellectual companion, but after so many decades only an enemy in the end, an enemy of my ideas, an enemy of my thoughts, an enemy of my very existence, which is nothing other than an intellectual existence. I had written several letters to you in Vienna and Madrid, then in Budapest and Palermo, but letters never sent, all of these letters stamped and addressed, as a matter of fact, but not sent so as not to be a sacrifice to someone's bad taste. I have destroyed these letters and sworn never to write you another line, not one more to you or anyone else. I permitted myself no more correspondence. So I travelled throughout Europe and North America for several years, probably on a *vain whim* as you would say, without contacts, without correspondence, since my communicativeness suddenly went dead, after denying it to myself for years. I went *inside myself*, so to speak, and not *outside myself any more*. But I can't say that this time had been spent pointlessly. To be brief, I wrote several articles for the *Times*, which were not published, naturally, for I didn't send them to the *Times*, this after settling in Oslo in the truest sense of the word. Oslo is a boring city and the people there are unintellectual and perfectly uninteresting as likely all Norwegians are, this is an impression that I had much later, however, after I had gone as far up as Murmansk. Save that the food is bad and the Norwegians have terrible taste when it comes to art, I did learn about a breed of dog there, until now totally unknown in Central Europe, the so-called *Schaufler*. A perfectly unphilosophical country in which every kind of idea is smothered in the shortest time. I gave it a try at a nursing home in Mosjøen, a small city of poor people in which they dispel the boredom by playing a piano; supposedly every second family in Mosjøen has a piano, and I myself in the house where I spent my first night, or, better, *survived*, saw and heard a Bösendorfer grand which had been so out of tune that even the most insipid music by Schubert, for example, was interesting when played on it; with their out-of-tune pianos the people of Mosjøen, as I would assume Norwegians in general, have acquired a real notion of so-called *modern music today* more or less on their own since they have, as far as I can tell, no clue about it. But these Norwegian experiences, which have given me almost every hope for my future and which, during my counting of fur hats and felt clogs and felt boots and, as I said, the most perverse of every possibility of playing the piano, have in fact been exhausted, are not what makes me write these lines to you. I had a dream and since you are a dream collector, I don't want to keep from you this dream of mine that I dreamt in Rotterdam, for I am, as you know, an unconditional supporter and devotee of the arts and sciences, especially of yours, and I can easily set aside the utter coldness of our relationship and tell you about this dream that I dreamt in Rotterdam following my departure from Oslo, after spending some time in Lübeck, Kiel, and in the Hamburg railroad station, as well as a couple of weeks in disgusting Bruges—where I had another go at being a nurse as in Norway, an *insane asylum nurse* as a matter of fact—I had a dream *and I recalled it*, for I dream daily, as you know, but I don't recall all of these daily dreamt dreams. How few dreams of mine there are that I dream and recall! As you know, I have for many years been fleeing from Austria *to a better place than Austria* and I will never come back to Austria under any circumstances, as I think now, unless compelled to do so by force. So I travelled, or, better put, I wandered for years in Europe and here and there in North America, as you know, with the intention of finding a place in which I can realize my plans, my philosophically existential plans, about which I spoke to you so often and for so long until you couldn't stand it any more, especially in the South Tyrol, especially there in Ritten. Because I wanted to be neither an Oxford brain nor a Cambridge brain; above all, to especially endeavour to mightily keep away from every university is what I have always been telling myself in recent years, and, as you know, I have also avoided for years any books with academic content so as to avoid philosophy wherever I can, literature wherever I can, any kind of reading material in general wherever I can out of fear now, for this reading material is getting to be truly crazy and insane and ultimately deadening; hence the difficulties of travelling through Europe and North America. I always had the greatest fear of Asia and my journey to India ended in a total fiasco as well, as you know, since I am, as you know, of a weaker physical constitution. And Latin America has become very fashionable, yet what repels me is that everyone in Europe goes and imposes themselves there under this mantle of social and socialist cooperation, which in reality is nothing but a disgusting subspecies of European Christian-Socialist fussiness. The Europeans bore themselves to death and meddle everywhere in the so-called *Third World* in order to escape that fatal European boredom. Missionarianism is a German vice which has invariably just brought misfortune to the world today, which has invariably just plunged the world into crisis. The Church has only poisoned Africa with its detestable *dear God*, and now it is poisoning Latin America with it. The Catholic Church is the world poisoner, the world destroyer, the world annihilator, that is the truth. The Germans continually poison the world outside of their borders and they will give it no rest until this entire world is fatally poisoned. So I have long withdrawn from my *bad* habit of wanting to help people in Africa and South America and into myself entirely. There is no helping humanity in our world which has been a hypocrisy for centuries. And, like humanity, there is no helping the world because both *are* a hypocrisy through and through. But this you surely know about me and this isn't what it's about. The fact is that I simply want to write and tell you about what I dreamt today because it will be useful to you, I think. I dreamt of Austria with such intensity because I have escaped from Austria as though it were from the ugliest and most absurd country on earth. Everything that the people of this country always have seen as beautiful and admirable was just uglier and more absurd, evermore repugnant, and I found not a single iota in this Austria which was ever acceptable. I felt my country to be a perverse wasteland, one of appalling dullness. Only gruesome, mutilated cities, nothing but a forbidding landscape, and in these mutilated cities and forbidding landscape, a vulgar and hypocritical and vile people. It wasn't realizing *what* so mutilated these cities, so desolated this land, made these people so vulgar and vile. The landscape was as vulgar as the people, as mutilated, as mean, one was just as forbidding as the other in a totally fatal way, you must realize. If I saw people, they only wore vulgar devil masks where they should have had a face, if I opened newspapers, I had to vomit over the stupidity and vileness inside, everything I saw, everything I heard, everything that I had to see made me nauseous. I was doomed for weeks on end seeing and hearing this despicable Austria, you must know, until I was finally reduced to a skeleton of despair from this fatal hearing and seeing; I could no longer eat a bite because of my aversion to this Austria, I could no longer take a sip. Wherever I looked, I saw only ugliness and vulgarity, an ugly and hypocritical and vulgar nature and an ugly and vulgar and hypocritical people, the absolute filthiness and vulgarity and vileness of these people. And don't think that I only saw the government and the so-called upper class as such, everything Austrian was at once the ugliest, the stupidest, the most repulsive. In *seriously damaged condition*, as you might say, I sat down, after I had run through this ugly and vulgar and stupid Austria several times in my breathless way, you must realize, I sat down on a block of conglomerate stone on Salzburg's Haunsberg where I— totally jaded by its inhabitants and totally destroyed by the architecture of your colleagues, but still in their perverse obsession with size—looked down on that seething city of Salzburg. What have the Austrian people made of this European jewel in just forty or fifty years, I thought, sitting on this block of conglomerate stone? A single architectural abomination in which the Salzburgers, Catholic and National Socialist haters of Jews and immigrants, race back and forth in their gruesome Lederhosen and Loden cape costumes by the tens of thousands. On this block of conglomerate stone on Salzburg's Haunsberg I must have dozed off, so to speak, from world fatigue, sir, then I suddenly woke up on Vienna's Kahlenberg. And imagine, my dear architect and building artist, what I happened to see from the Kahlenberg after I woke up, no longer sitting on a block of conglomerate stone as on Salzburg's Haunsberg but on a rotten wooden bench over the so-called Himmelstrasse: this entire disgusting, ultimately just awful, reeking Austria, with all its vulgar and mean people, and with its world-famous churches and cloisters and theatres and concert halls, going up in flames and burning down before my eyes. By holding my nose, but with wide-open eyes and ears and a monstrous desire for immediate sensation, I saw it slowly burn to the ground and with the greatest possible theatrical effect on me, I saw it burning down so long until it was at first a yellow-black, then a grey-black plain of sticky ash, nothing else. And as I saw the remains of the Austrian government, which, as you know, has always been the stupidest government on earth, and the remains of the Austrian Catholic clergy, which has always been the most cunning on earth, as well as the barely recognizable remains of Christian-Socialism and Catholicism and National Socialism in that stinking grey-black desert of fire, I breathed a sigh of relief, albeit coughing. I breathed such a sigh of relief that I woke up. To my great happiness in Rotterdam, in this city that is so nearest and dearest to me of any city and for all sorts of reasons, as you know. Even though this absurd Austria hasn't been worth discussing in any way for many decades now, it is still rather interesting, especially for you, sir, I would think, that even I dreamt of it again after so many decades.

Notes

Goethe Dies (*Goethe schtirbt*)

First appeared in *Die Zeit* (19 March 1982)

Written to mark the 1982 sesquicentennial of the death of the great German poet, novelist, playwright, natural scientist, philosopher, statesman, etc., Johann Wolfgang von Goethe (1749–1832). The original title is in the Frankfurt Hessian dialect spoken by Goethe.

Page 3

Friedrich Wilhelm *Riemer* (1774–1845): German scholar, literary historian and factotum of Goethe.

Page 4

Friedrich Theodor *Kräuter* (1790–1856): Goethe's secretary.

The Doubting and the Doubting Nothing: An imaginary expression after sceptical philosophy which could also be translated as *that which is an aporia and that which is not an aporia*, an *aporia* being a state of logical impasse or contradiction where the only consideration ends in doubt. Bernhard (the 'doubting Thomas', as it were) derives this expression from Proposition 6.51 of the *Tractatus Logico-philosophicus* by Ludwig Wittgenstein:

Scepticism is not irrefutable, but palpably senseless, if it would doubt where a question cannot be asked.

For doubt can only exist where there is a question; a question only where there is an answer, and this only where something can be said.

The premise of the short story, indeed any fiction, flows from this idea as does the reliability of language in general.

Tractatus Logico-philosophicus: A seminal work of twentieth-century philosophy by Ludwig Wittgenstein (1889–1951), which amounted to 75 pages. The conceit here, in addition to the obvious one, is that such a small book dwarfs Goethe's entire opus, including his verse play *Faustus* (1808). That this book does so too, perhaps, should not be lost on the reader.

Goethe had been compelled for a lifetime to observe and record as Here . . . : The phenomenological way of expressing Goethe's method of scientific observation through intuitive perception and mentation has, perhaps, revealed to him his status vis-à-vis Wittgenstein.

Page 5

Johann Peter *Eckermann* (1792–1854): Poet and one of Goethe's secretaries. He is the author of *Conversations with Goethe* (*Gespräche mit Goethe*, 1836–48).

Frauenplan: literally, 'Women's Square'. In Weimar, it is the location of Goethe's townhouse and last residence. The irony here is that Goethe's house is staffed by so many female servants, a virtual chorus.

Christoph Martin *Wieland* (1733–1813): Poet, also resided in Weimar.

Friedrich *Schiller* (1759–1805): Goethe's rival and collaborator. He had lived in a townhouse nearby on the Esplanade.

Page 11

Oxford or Cambridge: To Goethe, are one and the same place; he virtually confuses them and where Wittgenstein really resides. The *Channel* is the English Channel.

Bedlam: From the equivalent *Bethel*, the common name for many historic German asylums.

dahlia: A botanist and natural scientist, Goethe was fond of dahlias and grew various hybrids in his Weimar garden. They played a part in his theory of the metamorphosis of natural beings and a cultivar is named in his honour.

Page 12

Arthur *Schopenhauer* (1788–1860): German philosopher.

Adalbert *Stifter* (1805–68): Austrian writer and painter.

Cornelia Schellhorn (1668–1754): Goethe's paternal grandmother.

Katharina Elisabeth Schulltheiss (1731–1808): Goethe's mother, however her maiden name is given incorrectly here. It is Textor, the Latin equivalent of Weber. If the uncertainties are deliberate—for Cornelia Schellhorn is more likely Goethe's beloved sister Cornelia—the narrator and his interlocutor are revealed as being less than expert about Goethe's life.

Ernst August II Konstantin (1737–58): Duke of Saxe-Weimar and Eisenach, a patron of Goethe's father, Johann Caspar Goethe (1710–82).

Page 13

Ulrike Levetzow (1804–99): A young noble woman who rejected Goethe's marriage proposal when she was only 17 and he 73, a disappointment that led Goethe to write his most famous poem, 'Marienbad Elegy'.

Charlotte *von Stein* (1742–1827): Salonist, whose circle of friends included Schiller and Goethe.

Heinrich von *Kleist* (1777–1811): German writer.

Johann Gottfried von *Herder* (1744–1803): German philosopher, theologian and poet.

In the wind snick the weathervanes: Closing line of the poem 'Hälfte des Lebens' (Half of Life) by Friedrich Hölderlin.

Page 14

Thomaskantor: That is, Johann Sebastian Bach (1685–1750), who once served as cantor of the Thomasschule in Leipzig.

Page 15

Suhrkamp Library: Founded in 1951, reissued a series of classics in inexpensive bindings, including Wittgenstein's *Tractatus Logico-philosophicus*. Bernhard is describing his first copy of the book.

Page 16

The tautology has no truth-conditions . . . : Proposition 4.461 of the *Tractatus*.

Elenbogen: German name of Loket, Czech Republic. Here Goethe spent his seventy-fourth birthday depressed over the failure of his marriage proposal to Ulrike Levetzow.

Edith Lafontaine: Fictitious name

Voltaire (i.e. François-Marie Arouet, 1694–1778): French philosopher, long dead.

Hotel Pupp: The present-day Grand Hotel Karlovy Vary when it was under the ownership of Julius Pupp (1870–1936).

Page 18

Gickelhahn: Literally, 'cockerel'. A mountain near Ilmenau, where Goethe had written his famous lyric 'Über allen Gipfeln is Ruh' (Over All the Mountaintops Is Peace) on the wall of a hunter's hut there in 1780. The admiration for this eight-line poem made it a cliché even in Goethe's lifetime.

Page 21

Elephant: On Weimar's Marktplatz Square, the Hotel Zum Elefantan, one of Germany's most famous hotels. Founded in 1696, virtually every notable from the early modern period to the present has stayed there. Today, golden statues are often placed on the hotel's famous main balcony to celebrate its famous guests, such as Schiller, Goethe, Liszt, Wagner, Alma Mahler and Walter Gropius, even Elvis Presley—all save Hitler.

Montaigne: A Story in Twenty-Two Instalments

(*Montaigne. Eine Erzählung in 22 Fortsetzungen*)

First appeared in *Die Zeit* (8 October 1982).

Originally written for the feuilleton of *Die Zeit* and to inaugurate a new series of so-called miniature serial novels (*Miniatur-Fortsetzung-Romane*) contained in a single issue—this being an antidote to readers exhausted by the time commitment of reading the newspaper's literary supplements leading up to the Frankfurt Book Fair. Bernhard, a natural comedian, supplied the first text, which played off his reputation for writing 'breathless narratives in hundreds of pages without a single paragraph' by his marking up the manuscript of 'Montaigne' into 22 paragraphs—the 'instalments'.

Page 25

Michel de *Montaigne* (1533–92): Philosopher, sceptic, essayist of the French Renaissance who also wrote extensively on the education of children. Like the narrator, Montaigne had a library attached to a tower.

Page 29

Neukirchen am *Enknach* . . . *Rutzenmoos*: Small towns near Salzburg in Upper Austria.

loneliness of Schopenhauer: An allusion to various observations made by Arthur Schopenhauer on the virtues and vicissitudes of solitude—from *Parerga and Paralipomena* (1851):

The less necessity there is for you to come into contact with mankind in general, in the relations whether of business or of personal intimacy, the better off you are.

*[S]olitude is the sole condition of life that gives full play to
the feeling of exclusive importance that every man has in his
own eyes—as if he were the only person in the world!*

Reunion (*Wiedersehen*)

First appeared in *Zeitgeist. Katalog zur Internationalen Kunst-
ausstellung Berlin 1982* (Berlin: Martin Gropius Bau, 1982), pp.
62–70.

Page 47

Giovanni *Segantini* (1858–99): Italian painter known for pas-
toral, Alpine landscapes and symbolist paintings, such as *The
Bad Mothers* (1894).

Ferdinand *Hodler* (1853–1916): Swiss, also known for his
Alpine genre paintings and symbolist style that he called
'Parallelism'.

Ferdinand Georg *Waldmüller* (1793–1865): Austrian genre
painter of the Biedermeier period.

Page 48

Ortler . . . the Matterhorn: Famous peaks and massifs of the
Southern Alps.

Page 49

Engadin: Valley in the Swiss Alps.

Page 53

Merano . . . the Toten Gebirge: Placenames and mountain-
climbing destinations in the Southern and Eastern Alps.

Page 55

Glockner Glacier: That is, the Grossglockner-Gletscher, Austria's highest mountain.

Novalis poems: In the fourth section of his *Hymns to the Night*, is the following: '[H]e who has stood on the mountain frontier of the world, . . . [o]n those heights he builds for himself tabernacles of peace . . . .'

Page 66

Schwarzach-Sankt Veit: Town near Salzburg on the Tauern Railway.

Flims: Town in the Glarus Alps of Switzerland.

Going Up in Flames: A Travelogue to an Erstwhile Friend

(*In Flammen aufgegangen. Reisebericht an einen einstigen Freund*)

First appeared in *Programmheft 52*, *Der Schein trügt* (Schauspielhaus Bochum, 1983–84), pp. 98–103.

Page 69

architect . . . building artist: A difference exists between these seemingly redundant appellations. In the postmodern period, a building artist (*Baukünstler*) connotes a visionary, forward-thinking architect as opposed to a mere certified professional.

Page 71

Schaufler: Literally, 'shoveller'. The German does not correlate with any known breed of dog specific to Norway. However, given the satirically disparaging context of this passage, it may mean the Norwegians themselves and a common

sight during the Norwegian winter of having to shovel and
dig out of the snow.

Mosjøen: Small industrial city in northern Norway.

Bösendorfer: A grand piano manufactured in Austria which features extended keyboards.

Page 72

Ritten: Commune in South Tyrol.

Page 75

Haunsberg: A hill and scenic overlook north of Salzburg.

Kahlenberg: A hill south of Vienna that offers a view of the entire city.

Himmelstrasse: Literally, 'Road to Heaven'. An avenue that passes through the Vienna Woods in the suburb of Grinzing.